THE WA

I promise to be a good student,

to feed my mind,

to strengthen my body,

to have truth in my heart,

to be kind and always do my best.

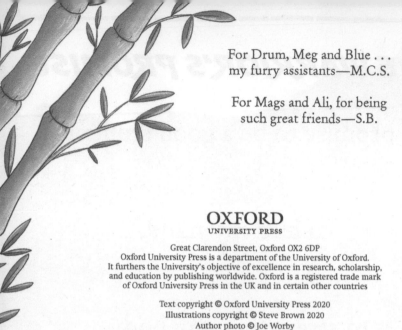

For Drum, Meg and Blue . . .
my furry assistants—M.C.S.

For Mags and Ali, for being
such great friends—S.B.

OXFORD
UNIVERSITY PRESS

Great Clarendon Street, Oxford OX2 6DP
Oxford University Press is a department of the University of Oxford.
It furthers the University's objective of excellence in research, scholarship,
and education by publishing worldwide. Oxford is a registered trade mark
of Oxford University Press in the UK and in certain other countries

Text copyright © Oxford University Press 2020
Illustrations copyright © Steve Brown 2020
Author photo © Joe Worby

The moral rights of the author have been asserted

Database right Oxford University Press (maker)

First published 2020

British Library Cataloguing in Publication Data

Data available

ISBN 978-0-19-277173-5

WARRIOR MONKEYS
MONKEYS
AND THE RESCUE Quest

M.C. STEVENS
ILLUSTRATED BY STEVE BROWN

OXFORD
UNIVERSITY PRESS

MEET THE CHARACTERS

SUKI

BEKKO

FARA

CHAN

SENSEI
RIKA

JIRUGI

MING

PROLOGUE

Miserable and freezing, the elephant dragged a stack of firewood across the courtyard. Hail battered her weary body. She was stiff with the cold, sore from the work, and irritated by the weasel jabbing her with his stick to keep her moving.

'Hatti! Hurry up!' the weasel snapped. 'The Emperor must be kept warm.' Hatti sighed to herself. She had been a slave to Emperor Ming since being kidnapped from her family when she was very young. She knew about being bullied. She knew about working from dawn to dusk. She knew about being sad. But she couldn't remember ever being warm.

She delivered the stack of logs to the Great Hall, and noticed that Emperor Ming had a visitor. The emperor himself, a giant panda, sat lazily on his comfortable throne by the biggest brazier in the room. His visitor, a large mandrill, had been given a smaller chair. It was still one of the better seats, however, so the elephant thought the guest must be quite important. She was not much interested though. It only meant she would be expected to fetch even more wood, so she began to plod back towards the forest before the weasel started jabbing her again.

Back in the Great Hall a new alliance was being formed.

'Your Imperial Majesty, thank you for granting me an audience. Your power is known through many countries. It is a great pleasure to meet you.' The mandrill, Jirugi, bowed respectfully to the panda who was clearly flattered by the compliments.

'Through many countries, eh? Glad to hear it! My family has ruled these mountains for many centuries but times are hard now. We are losing distant territories every year. My army and navy are nothing compared to the mighty forces commanded by my father.' Ming's voice was peevish and resentful. 'Creatures these days are weak in body and mind. No commitment! No loyalty! But you tell me you have a solution to this?'

'Yes, Your Highness. I come from the Shanti Islands, where warriors are trained in combat and strength from a very young age. I believe that with their methods, we could build an army strong enough for you to regain all seven mountain kingdoms.' Jirugi's bold claim was enough to make Ming sit up in his throne and drop his bamboo shoots. First he looked eager. Then he looked suspicious.

'What's in it for you? Why would you
help me?

'I think we can help each other. I need
an army to take over the Shanti Islands.
If we create an army together to conquer
the islands, then I won't need it any
more. It will be all yours and you can
restore your family's empire.'

'I'm interested. But YOU have not

trained an army.' Ming leaned forward, pointing at Jirugi. 'YOU do not have an army. How do you propose to create this strong loyal force?'

'Well, Your Highness, what we need is someone who has experience and skills in training young warriors. What do you do when someone else has what you need?' Jirugi already knew the answer to this. It was the reason he had made the long hard journey to Ming's court.

'Well, I go and take it, of course.' Ming shrugged as if this should be obvious. Jirugi smiled with satisfaction. 'Exactly! You have a ship. I have a plan...'

CHAPTER ONE

The coast of Senshi Island was full of
caves, pools, and cliff ledges that were
perfect for the agile warrior monkeys
to play, swim, and explore. This sunny
day saw the adventurous Suki making
daredevil leaps into the calm water; while
Bekko, her more cautious friend, was
looking for coloured pebbles along the
shore. He was accompanied by Ishi, his
loyal dog, who was happily jumping in

and out of the waves. He barked every time Suki went underwater, and wagged his tail energetically each time she reappeared.

Suki splashed her way out of the sea and came to join them. 'Come and swim, Bekko!' she said. 'The water is so clear today!'

'Later.' he promised. 'There's so much to see here in the rockpools. It's fascinating!'

She pointed into the distance. 'Chan seems more interested in the ocean, doesn't he?'

Chan, Senshi's wise old gardener, sat cross-legged on a distant rock. He was known for being able to meditate in strange places. He also seemed to know everything that went on in Senshi Castle despite the fact he had not been an official Guardian for many years. Suki thought he might be magical. But Bekko believed it was a combination of cleverness and observation. Although some of their friends took no notice of the old gardener, Suki and Bekko valued and respected him very highly. And it certainly was a wonderful day to look across the smooth ocean, unbroken except for a few distant boats on the horizon.

'Suki!' Bekko's stressed voice made her jump. 'Look at that catfish!'

She looked where he was pointing. The

fish seemed very agitated. It was joined by another, and another...all racing around the rock pool. Together they dived under the overhanging rocks.

'Are they hiding?' Suki asked. 'Why would they do that?'

Bekko had jumped on a ledge to look out towards the horizon. 'It can't be! It's so calm out there!'

'WHAT?' Suki demanded. 'It's really annoying when you think stuff without telling me!'

'Sorry! It doesn't make sense. Catfish get upset when there is going to be a tidal wave. But look at the weather! How can there be a tidal wave coming?' Bekko was gazing at the sky now, but there were no clouds and still only the lightest breeze.

'Erm, Bekko?' Suki grabbed his arm and pulled him to face the south. 'Look!'

He had never seen anything like it. The flat, peaceful ocean had grown a narrow bump. The bump was getting bigger. Tall and terrifying, it gained height rapidly and was heading directly towards them.

They looked at each other desperately.
What to do?

Suki knew the caves wouldn't be safe.
'Cliff path?'

'Yes, quick! Ishi! Here!' Bekko grabbed
his dog and together they sped towards
the path that led back to the castle.

'Behind these bushes?' Bekko gasped.
If they had something to hold onto,
perhaps they wouldn't be swept away.

'OK! You hold Ishi, I'll hold you! It's
going to hit!' Suki braced herself and
shut her eyes. Like a clap of thunder,
the strange wall of water smashed into
the cove as Suki took a deep breath. A
sudden shocking smash of water hit . . .
then tried to drag them into the ocean as

it surged back. They were pulled through the bushes, ending up drenched, choking, and stunned.

Bekko was unable to hang onto the wriggling, panicking dog any longer. Ishi chased the wave back towards the sea, barking indignantly. Suki sat up, rubbing her head.

'Are you OK?' Bekko asked, helping her to her feet.

'Something hit me,' she grimaced. 'I don't know what. But I'm OK. What on earth happened? That was totally bizarre!'

'I know!' he agreed. 'The weirdest thing! That was no ordinary wave. But it was far too narrow to be a tidal wave. Did it only hit this beach?'

She could only shrug helplessly. 'No idea, I was too busy trying not to drown! Where's Ishi?'

'He ran after it! Better go and find him.' Together, they made their way through the debris back down to the cove. Ishi was still barking at the sea. 'I think he's trying to tell it not to come back.' Bekko remarked, observing the intensity and fury of the dog.

'Looks like it's gone, anyway,' said Suki, looking around at the scene. All was still again. They were surrounded by broken branches and could see water was cloudy with rocks, sand, and seaweed. But the sea was flat, the wave had gone as suddenly as it had appeared.

'Bekko, what about Chan?' Suki was suddenly very alarmed. 'Do you think he had time to get to safety?'

'Oh, good grief! He's nowhere to be seen!' Bekko leapt up again to scan the horizon, but this time nothing was approaching. And Chan's rock was absolutely, definitely empty.

Suki immediately dived into the murky sea. Maybe Chan was hurt. Maybe he was holding on to a rock or some debris and they could rescue him. Her heart was in her mouth as she pulled herself on to the rock. And then it fell. For there was a soggy book of Chan's favourite meditations stuck in a crevice. And no Chan . . . anywhere.

CHAPTER TWO

The dripping and bedraggled Suki and
Bekko finished their dramatic report
to Sensei Rika, the Guardian of Senshi
Castle. Always calm and purposeful, she
listened to their tale without interruption
and decided there was no need to panic.
'I'm not worried about Chan,' she said.
'He may just be headed further up the
coast for some peace and quiet.'

'But Sensei!' Bekko was very agitated.

'It really was a very weird wave; what if it has pulled him right out to sea?'

Sensei Rika patted him on the shoulder. 'Chan is a very strong swimmer, Bekko. He could easily swim all the way over to Silla if he wanted to. I'm sure there's no need to worry about him.'

'I wish you had seen it, Sensei,' Suki said earnestly. 'I know it doesn't sound really bad, but I've never seen anything like it.'

'I can see you're worried. But it's training time now. I'm sure Chan will be home soon. Now get tidied up; I'll see you in the training hall after warm up.' Rika dismissed them. Suki and Bekko had no choice but to hurry up and get themselves to class.

Suki did her best to steady her head as she started her warm up with the other cadets. As a young student she was easily distracted. Now, however, she took pride in controlling her focus. She began to work on her defence patterns; traditional sequences of movement like a solo battle. The power and rhythm of the steps took all her concentration; she found her mind settling into the present and leaving behind the rough sea and the disappearance of Master Chan. Smooth, strong, and balanced ... she blocked, twisted, punched, and threw her invisible opponents with control and determination.

Bekko had chosen to work on strength exercises for his warm up. Twenty long leaps, twenty press-ups, twenty high leaps, twenty press-ups: a tough routine he had learned from the strongest monkeys in the group. Nita and Lili liked to compete to see who could finish their sets first. Kang and Yash preferred to take

turns to count repetitions and motivate
each other.

Kang was yelling at Yash. 'Come on!
Get your chin down on those press-ups!
Flat back! No cheating! That's it! Four
more to go! Seventeen, eighteen, nineteen,
TWENTY!' Yash finished his sets then he
and Kang swapped places with a high five.

Meanwhile, Nita and Lili had completed their race—Nita narrowly ahead. She stopped to stretch while Lili went to join Suki with her defence patterns. Kang began his leaps. Yash marked out the longest jump with a stick so Kang could aim further every time. Bekko was beside them, trying to imitate Nita's run back to her starting point, leaving no recovery between jumps. His legs were wobbly at the end of the set but he flung himself down into twenty perfect press-ups then immediately raced into the high jumps. By the time he had completed the last press-ups, Bekko's arms and legs felt like they were on fire and he was panting heavily.

'You shouldn't rush like that.' Kang scolded Bekko, as he walked back to his starting line. 'You won't get stronger if you hurry through the sets. Take your time, and hit the range.' He shook his legs and set himself for another big effort with some deep breaths.

Kang could do more press-ups than any of the others, but his jumping was slow and heavy with a long recovery between each jump.

'You're wrong, Kang.' Nita cut in across Bekko, who was ready to ask Kang about his methods. 'Your way takes so long! Lili and I get our warm up done so much more efficiently.'

Kang shrugged. 'Whatever you think,

Nita. But I think you'll agree I'm stronger than you are.'

She was having none of it. 'Your arms are stronger. But I can kick a lot harder than you can! And run faster!' It was true, and he knew it. There was an awkward silence while Nita tapped her foot and waited for Kang to apologize.

'Strong arms are more important, anyway.' Yash interjected, wanting to defend his big friend. Kang grinned at him and did a couple of handstand press-ups, knowing Nita would be unimpressed.

Bekko tried to be diplomatic. 'I think you are both really fit and strong. We don't all have to have the same skills.'

'Choose to see the good!' Sensei Rika had overheard their conversation as she entered the dojo. 'Kang can punch hard. Nita can kick hard . . . both can be useful. It doesn't mean one is better than the other.'

They listened respectfully as she continued. 'The goal is to be the best version of yourself, and keep improving no matter how you choose to do it. Now, pair up, and let's work on your sparring!'

After a hard session of sparring, Suki and Bekko were tired and hungry. However, their strange experience on the beach and their concern for Chan meant they waited to speak to Sensei Rika at the end of the session instead of running off to get their dinner.

'Sensei, is there any news about Chan?' Bekko asked, anxiously.

'Not yet. Try not to worry. He's probably fine.' Sensei Rika's words were reassuring but Suki thought she could detect worry in her face. Their heads and spirits were low as they left the training hall. A distant knock on the castle gate, however, had them all springing to attention.

'The gate!' Bekko exclaimed. 'Could it be Chan?'

'Let's go and see,' said Sensei Rika, sweeping ahead across the courtyard. Suki had a horrible feeling of nervous anticipation as she jogged along with the others. Nothing had seemed right since that unnatural wave.

Bekko caught up with her and hissed in her ear. 'I don't like this, Suki. Does this feel wrong to you?'

'Definitely,' she whispered back. 'I hope we're both mistaken. Maybe it really is just Chan coming back.' But the person returning to Senshi Castle was one they had never expected to see again in their whole lives. Standing in the gatehouse, drenched and ragged, was a small snub-nosed monkey.

'YUNNAN!' burst out Suki and Bekko together. 'What are you doing here?'

'This is Yunnan?' snapped Sensei Rika.

'He works for Jirugi, doesn't he?'

'I've run away, Sensei. Actually, I jumped overboard.' Now the little monkey was kneeling. 'Please, Sensei Rika, I'm so sorry to disturb you with bad news. Jirugi has kidnapped Chan.'

Sensei Rika ignored the gasps around her. She studied Yunnan carefully. 'I see. I think you had better come in.'

In the council chamber, the little monkey looked very awkward and out-of-place. At first, he refused to sit down. Then he refused any food.

'Come along, Yunnan.' Sensei Rika encouraged. 'Have some tea. Suki and Bekko need to eat too. We can eat and talk. I'm guessing you must be hungry.'

Poor Yunnan didn't know what to do. He was starving after his long swim. However, Jirugi always treated him like a filthy and unwanted servant, not a guest.

'But Sensei, what if I am lying to you? What if I am a traitor? What if this is a trap?' he cried, pushing away the plate of nuts and seeds Suki had laid out for him.

'What if you are?' Sensei Rika shrugged. 'You still need to eat. You look weak. You don't need to be treated badly just because you are a prisoner. That's not our way.'

Yunnan looked as if he couldn't quite understand what he was hearing. However, he cautiously took a few nuts

and tried to eat them without making any
noise. Then he started to cry.

'No one has been kind to me since I
was taken from my mother. Lord Jirugi
shouts at me all day. I think I am a very
bad servant, he is never happy with my
work but I do try so hard!'

Bekko went to sit next to Yunnan and
comfort him. He always hated to see

anyone in distress. Of course, he was suspicious of Yunnan but he thought Sensei Rika was right to hear his story and make her own mind up. And unless he was proved to be a liar, he deserved to be trusted. Respect and courtesy were always important for Warrior Monkeys.

Suki was more impatient than Bekko and didn't feel that gentle behaviour was the right approach. She grabbed Yunnan's arm and pulled him to his feet. 'Where is Chan? How was he captured?'

His reply was instant but left her completely puzzled. 'Ming's ship. It was a Namazu.'

'Who is Ming? What is a Namazu? And where are they taking him? Is he

OK?' Now she was shaking his arm as she rushed through her questions.

'Suki. Let him tell us. Then we can ask questions.' Sensei Rika motioned to Suki to step back and they all sat down again. 'Yunnan, did Jirugi capture a Namazu?'

Yunnan nodded. 'Yes, Sensei. It wasn't full size. But it was big enough to wash him out to sea where we could capture him.'

This still made no sense to Suki, but for Bekko a light was dawning.

'The giant catfish! They make tidal waves, Suki! That's why the little catfish were going crazy.'

She looked amazed. 'I've never heard that! It sounds really scary!'

Rika put out a reassuring hand. 'Jirugi wouldn't be able to control a big one. They're mostly happy creatures who don't make any trouble. But if they are captured they get angry and they make the sea shake. But who is this Ming person, Yunnan?'

'Ming is the emperor of the seven kingdoms in the mountains beyond Gimandesh. His family used to be the most powerful in the world but now their army is weak and Ming cannot control all his territories. Lord Jirugi promised to help him build an army to get strong again.'

Rika raised her eyebrows. 'Oh no. Don't tell me Jirugi thinks he's going

to get Chan to train an enemy army.'
She started to laugh. 'Seriously? That's
ridiculous!'

Yunnan looked a little surprised at her
laughter. 'Jirugi will make him do it! He
won't have a choice!'

This made her chuckle even more. 'No
one can ever make Chan do something
he doesn't want to do. Especially if he
believes it is wrong.'

'Jirugi has promised Ming that Chan
can create a loyal and powerful team of
warriors. Strong enough to conquer the
Shanti Islands and take back the lands
Ming has lost.' Yunnan explained.

Again Rika smiled. 'Jirugi is absolutely
correct. Chan could do that. He won't

though! I wonder what Ming will say when it goes wrong.'

'Sensei? Isn't Chan in danger?' Bekko asked. 'If he refuses to help, they will surely kill him!'

She smiled at him. 'Chan doesn't see danger the same way that you do, Bekko. He won't be scared. He always has a plan. The only way they can keep him prisoner is if he chooses to stay. Perhaps he will stay long enough for them to regret the whole idea. Maybe they already do.'

Bekko looked unconvinced. He hated the idea of Chan being a prisoner.

'Where are they taking him, Yunnan?' asked Suki.

'To Ming's court in Mahala. It's in the

mountain tops where it is very cold. So
so cold! We went there for meetings. I
thought my toes were going to fall off.'
Yunnan shuddered. 'It is a very long trek.
Right into the sky. They will have to sail
for many days first though. Then climb
into the mountains.'

'I see. I have never heard of Mahala.
Warrior Monkeys rarely visit the
mountains in Gimandesh, let alone
beyond. Chan will have plenty to tell us
when he gets back.' Sensei Rika stood
as if to finish the meeting. 'Yunnan, we
appreciate you coming to tell us this.
Escaping must have been dangerous
for you. Swimming all the way to
shore must also have been very tough.

You are welcome to stay here in our community, I'm sure we can find work for you to do to earn your keep.'

Yunnan burst in tears again. 'Sensei, I can never repay your kindness. However, I am worried about Master Chan. Jirugi and Ming are bad men. I can't help him on my own but if we go together maybe we can save him!'

At last, this was something Suki could agree with. 'Yes, Sensei! I will go with him! I'm not scared of the mountains. Or the enemies!'

Bekko added his plea. 'Sensei, I can't lie. I am scared, but I can't rest until Chan is home. Surely we can go and help him?'

'It's not needed.' Sensei Rika was firm. 'Chan may be a captive but he's wily and clever. He can look after himself. You are young and inexperienced. People die in the mountains! They get lost. They fall. They give up and perish in the cold. I'm not risking my warriors. You stay here.' And with that, she dismissed them.

Suki drew herself up to argue, but Bekko nudged her to stop. He could see that Sensei Rika was not inclined to battle with them. Leaving Yunnan, they bowed out of the room.

CHAPTER THREE

After such an exhausting day, Suki slept well but she woke very early. The thought of Chan being carried off to Mahala really bothered her and she couldn't get back to sleep. Quietly, she took her backpack and sneaked along to Bekko's room. If Sensei Rika would not give them permission to go after Chan, then maybe they would just have to go without any permission. It would be hard to persuade Bekko to break the rules though. Perhaps she could catch him when he was still sleepy and get him to agree before he properly woke up.

But Bekko's room was empty. There were the usual rows of pebbles and piles of books and maps. If Suki knew more about Bekko's book collection she would have noticed some important history books were missing. She didn't spend

any time checking the shelves though; she was keen to track down Bekko before everyone else was up. Otherwise gathering food and equipment for an expedition would definitely arouse suspicion.

She guessed that Bekko might be in the grounds with Ishi and sure enough she found him in the zen garden. He was leaning on his dog and studying a huge book, notebook in hand. Ishi looked up sharply as Suki approached. He usually made a fuss when anyone came close to Bekko, but Suki was an exception. Bekko brightened when he saw Suki and shut his book. He was about to speak when Suki blurted her plan.

'Let's sneak out and look for Chan. If we pretend we're just going for a swim we can go and find a boat heading for Gimandesh.'

He started to object. 'No, but ...'

'I know you want to help him too!'

'Yes, but ...'

'Sensei Rika will understand we had to go!'

'No, but ...'

'Chan might be in serious danger!'

'Yes, but ...'

'We can't just stay here!'

'SUKI, LISTEN!' Bekko snapped, exasperated. 'I've found the answer. It's right here. Sensei Rika can't stop us doing this.' Ishi jumped up and barked.

'Can't stop you doing what?' came a familiar voice from behind them. Sensei Rika appeared from the kitchen garden.

'Yes, WHAT?' demanded Suki.

Bekko knelt down in front of Sensei Rika and bowed very formally.

'Sensei,' he said, 'as a warrior cadet, I invoke the right to undertake a Taiku Quest.'

She looked surprised. Disconcerted even. 'I see. Well, if you must, I have to hear your plan.' Sensei Rika knelt in return and bowed to Bekko. Suki had no idea what was going on but managed to stay quiet. Bekko certainly looked like he knew what he was doing.

'Justify your quest and surrender your

weapon,' Rika instructed.

Bekko reached for his stick and laid it on the ground.

'I will travel far to help others despite danger. I will take no money and no weapon. I will suffer hardship without complaint. I will go peacefully in the spirit of Senshi Castle.'

'Name your companion.' Sensei Rika responded.

'I name Suki.'

'Your quest cannot be refused. But you know that this right has not been invoked for over one hundred years. Few return from a Taiku Quest to claim their belt. Do you reconsider?'

'Sensei, my quest is not for the belt.

My quest is to find Chan. I believe in my heart that this is my duty as a warrior. I claim it.' Bekko met the Sensei's steady gaze without flinching.

Rika inclined her head respectfully and rose. 'Then I suggest you explain all this to Suki. It's not too late to change your mind. I urge you to reflect.' She left with a frown on her face, leaving Suki exploding with questions.

'Come on, Suki,' he said. 'We might as well have this conversation at Kuma's. And a good breakfast. We've got quite a journey ahead of us.'

'So, basically, the guardians used to award the blue belt of the warrior after the cadet had completed the Taiku Quest?' Suki was catching up with her history lesson, mouth full of banana bread.

Kuma nodded. 'And no guard bears could attend. No weapons, books, maps, or any help could be given from the castle because the quest is supposed to be about proving your independence.'

'But now they award the blue belt when you finish training here at Senshi Castle, before you go to work on the other islands. Why did that change?' Suki asked.

'Because it was just too dangerous,' Bekko explained. 'The guardians decided they didn't want to lose good warriors on an unnecessary mission. Warriors prove themselves with their service here on the islands. However, the right to claim the quest has never been removed. I knew I had read about it in one of my books.'

'I wish I could come with you.' Kuma said, sadly. 'I'll be worried about you.'

'I wish you could too,' Suki said, wrapping him in a big hug. 'We promise to be careful.'

'It's not the same as going to the other islands or trekking up the mountains here.' Kuma pointed out. 'How will you find your way? And what if you get attacked? You don't know what creatures are out there!'

'No, we don't,' agreed Bekko. 'But I've got Suki and she's got me. We will help each other. And at least we can tell you where we are going. I won't be able to explain it to Ishi. What am I going to do about him?' He looked out of Kuma's window where Ishi was lying under a bush. He felt terrible that he was going to have to leave his dog behind.

Suki leaned against Bekko sympathetically. 'What about asking Ko to look after him?' They both knew the littlest monkey was a kind soul, even though he was quite scared of Ishi.

'Maybe. It's hard for Ishi to trust anyone.'

Yet as they watched, a solution seemed to present itself almost magically. Yunnan arrived, obviously heading towards Kuma's rooms. As Ishi looked up, instead of growling, he wagged his tail. Noticing the dog, Yunnan knelt down with delight and encouraged him to approach. Ishi rushed at him and started to lick his face with excitement. Bekko and Suki looked at each other amazed. They had never seen Ishi behave like that with anyone other than Bekko.

'Well,' said Kuma. 'That makes me feel like I can trust Yunnan.'

'Because Ishi likes him?' Suki asked.

Bekko had followed Kuma's reasoning all the way. 'Not just that, Suki, but remember that Jirugi had Ishi as a puppy. I'm guessing Yunnan was kind to him, even though Jirugi was cruel.'

'Ohhhhh,' Suki smiled, pleased to see this evidence for Yunnan's honesty and kindness. She always believed in Ishi's instincts. 'Let's go and talk to him.'

Yunnan looked up as they emerged from the gatehouse. 'Ah! I was looking for you! Sensei Rika told me you are going. She won't let me come with you though. I want to tell you all I can about Ming and Jirugi before you go.'

'Thank you. We have a lot of questions!' Bekko replied fervently. 'First, I have a big favour to ask you though.'

'Anything!' Little Yunnan looked keen to be of service. 'What can I do to help you?'

'It's about my dog . . .'

Later that same morning, Bekko and Suki said goodbye to their home and their friends. Suki could not hide her excitement as she raced down the hill towards the harbour. She did not look back at the row of faces at the gate. Sensei

Rika's was serious. Kuma was sad, proud, and anxious. Yunnan had his arm around Ishi, who whined as Bekko tore himself away and followed Suki.

Choking back tears, Bekko stumbled along the path. Leaving Ishi, leaving Senshi Castle, leaving everything that was familiar . . . he was terrified and overwhelmed. His heart beat loudly in his chest and his lungs hurt. Was he sniffing, or was he gasping? He barely knew.

'Focus, Bekko'. The voice in his head was his own. But it was also the dear voice of Chan. How many times had Chan helped him to calm his distress? And Chan was the reason he was doing this. They had to try and rescue him!

The idea helped to settle him
as he caught up with Suki.
She was jumping aboard
the little boat that would
ferry them to Lanka.
He sat next to her as
Captain Uma cast
off and set the
sails.

'Oh, Bekko!' Suki saw his tears and gave him a huge hug. 'Are you sure about this?' Excited as she was, she knew that this was a huge step for her timid friend. Maybe he regretted his suggestion and felt he couldn't back out now.

'Thanks, Suki. I'll be OK. Give me a few minutes.' She squeezed his arm and left him to himself. He sat tall, took deep breaths, and looked away from Senshi island. Staring at the horizon, he imagined Chan as a prisoner. 'We're coming for you, Master Chan' he whispered to the sea.

CHAPTER FOUR

On the big dock at Lanka, they waved
goodbye to Uma and began to walk along
the piers, looking at traders. As they had
no money and nothing to trade with,
they intended to stow away on a suitable
ship.

'That one?' Suki suggested, pointing at
a tall ship which was being loaded with
cargo. They could see sacks of nuts and
charcoal as well as crates of bananas: the

usual exports taken to Gimandesh by trading ships.

'Looks good!' Bekko agreed. It was one of the biggest ships, so hopefully it would be easy for them to hide. Baboons were carrying crates up gangplanks at the front, middle, and back of the decks.

'Let's go up the other side. Look, we can catch that rope there.' Suki pointed to where a line hung down towards the water. Waiting until the baboon closest to them was out of sight on the deck, they swung below the jetty and leapt over to grab the line. A rapid climb was no trouble with their monkey agility. Bekko reached the deck first and hid behind a barrel. Suki joined him and together they

considered their choices.

'Down the hatch as soon as that last crate is brought up?' Suki whispered. Bekko nodded. They watched the last of the bananas being lowered into the hold. Then counted under their breath together, nodding as they went.

'Three, two, one . . . go!' Down they scampered and huddled in an empty barrel underneath the hatch. Above them, there were steps and the hatch was closed with a bang.

'Hey! What do you think you're doing?' A loud voice burst across the deck. Who could have seen them? They were so careful! They held hands and froze. Then another voice could be heard replying.

'Sorry, boss! Didn't see there was more to come.' Light burst into the hold again as the hatch was opened.

'Oh no!' Bekko made a vomiting face. He could smell what was coming before it arrived. The empty barrel had been perfectly placed for the remaining cargo. The two monkeys found themselves buried under a ton of smelly fish. Luckily the hatch was immediately shut again, so they could pull themselves out.

'Slimy. Smelly. Grooooooossssssssss!' squirmed Bekko. Suki couldn't help giggling.

'Your worst nightmare, Bekko! Well, hey, if the worst has already happened, then everything from here will be fine!'

He smiled wryly in response. They could feel the ship slipping from its mooring and departing for the open sea. Whatever was ahead, they both thought it was probably worse than a fishy shower.

It didn't take long for them to get used to being at sea. For Suki, the worst part was staying inside hiding instead of enjoying her usual freedom to leap and run. She did her best to make obstacle courses and mazes with the cargo, getting Bekko to time her as she ran through, or into, the dark pathways.

Bekko found the constant rocking

motion very soothing. He spent most of his time trying to remember things. He tried to keep Suki occupied with quizzes and fun facts as they spent the days and nights listening to the crew above. Several days passed in which nothing really happened. Even Bekko wasn't sure how long it would take to arrive though, so they were both surprised and hopeful when one day there was a lot of noise on the deck, and the ship swung to a sudden stop.

'Oooooh, that was quicker than I thought it would be!' Suki was jumping in excitement. 'I wonder how long it will be until we can sneak off? When will they start unloading?'

'Hold on,' Bekko put a restraining hand on her arm. 'Listen. Those are not dock noises. I think we're under attack!'

Scuffling. Shouting. And then the most bizarre whooping noise.

'Ooooowahoooooowaooooowaaaaa!' Over and over again! An intense noise they had never heard before; melodic, but insistent. Judging by the cries of the crew above, whatever was making the noise was definitely not friendly.

'What is THAT?' Suki's immediate reaction was to ask Bekko, who always knew everything. In this case though, he was just as baffled as she was. They could hear the unmistakable noises of close-range fighting happening above.

Crashes, hollers, battle cries, and flurries of footsteps . . . Suki found it very hard to stay still while a battle was in progress.

'Don't you think we should go and help the crew?' she urged Bekko. 'We can't just sit here.'

'Depends who is attacking them,' he replied sensibly. 'What do you know about Gimandesh's enemies?'

'Erm. Nothing.' Suki admitted.

'Exactly. We don't know who is the good side or the bad side here. We're just stowaways. We need to wait and see what happens.' Bekko climbed some crates to press his ear to the ceiling. 'I think it's over.'

And then the hatch was wrenched open.

Blinded by the sudden light, they both screwed up their eyes. They heard, but did not see, light feet landing around them. Hands grabbed strongly.

'Look, Rasmaya! What are these two doing down here?'

'Bring them up!'

And just like that . . . they were prisoners.

'Let go of me!' Struggling, shouting and trying to bite her captors, Suki was dragged up to the deck. Bekko, on the other hand, remained calm. He could feel how strong his captors were, he could see that he and Suki were heavily outnumbered, and he still wanted to find

out more before he assumed these were enemies.

By the time he stood on the deck, the invaders had tied and gagged Suki. In fairness, it was probably for everyone's safety that they did this. For himself, he had decided to act like Chan as much as he could: composed and aware of what was happening around them. Although scared, he was also intrigued; these were clearly pirates. He had heard stories about famous pirates raiding the waters close to Gimandesh but there was no way to tell what was history and what was just nonsense. This was definitely real. And it was definitely interesting.

The pirates looked quite like other monkeys Bekko knew from home, but they were bigger and they had very long arms. Some were swinging high above the deck, running along the masts and then making hanging leaps to their own ship alongside the trader. They were setting up connecting ropes in a very systematic and organized way. So Bekko's first impression was that they were well-trained as a team. He saw them lower a wide gangplank and then they began to empty the hold with its valuable cargo of food.

He could see the crew of the trader all

neatly tied together at the stern. Some had bruises and torn clothes; he assumed this was due to the fight. Many looked dazed or seemed to be rubbing bumps on their heads. From this, he concluded the pirates were not excessively violent and that they were skilled fighters. Controlling and capturing opponents without significantly injuring them was also a goal of the warrior monkeys. The ship had been conquered with the minimum necessary force, with speed and efficiency. These pirates were impressive.

The pirate leader stood in front of him. 'Who are you, and what are you doing here?' she demanded. Tall and athletic, she had natural authority. He

bowed politely. 'My name is Bekko, and my friend is called Suki. We are Warrior Monkeys from the Shanti Islands. And we are on a quest.'

'It must be an important quest. I hear the Shanti Islanders rarely venture abroad. You are young for such a responsibility.' She folded her arms and leaned against the mast, waiting for him to say more.

'One of our teachers has been kidnapped by an old enemy and we volunteered to go after him. We have no argument with you. Please allow us to continue our mission.' Bekko tried to stand tall despite being so much smaller than the pirate leader. He met her gaze without fear, and with as much truth as he could summon.

'If you have no argument with us then why is your friend attacking us?' The leader indicated the still-struggling Suki who was furious and frustrated.

'She's a warrior. She doesn't take kindly to being tied up. If you free her she will behave. If she doesn't, then tie me up too.' Bekko spoke confidently, though his glance at Suki was pleading. He was relieved to see a little nod from her.

'Somer, untie her' directed the pirate leader. Smoothly, the pirate holding Suki pulled the knots open and the friends were reunited.

'Thank you.' Bekko bowed again to the pirates. 'We won't trouble you further.'

'Hey, not so fast. What do you think will happen now?' The tall pirate was amused. 'Do you think these traders will let you stay with them? They're not usually very kind to stowaways. By the time we've taken their cargo, they won't be in the best mood to negotiate safe passage either. You'll be thrown overboard in no time.'

Behind her, the pirate crew was making a swift job of emptying the hold. Time was running out.

Suki took her turn to negotiate. 'It's true we're in danger. Maybe you can help us. We really need to get to Mahala: the court of Ming. We don't know how to get there. We don't even know where it is.'

'Ming!' the pirate leader choked. 'That evil tyrant! We would never help any friend of his!'

'No, no,' Suki hurried to explain. 'Ming is our enemy. He's the one who has kidnapped Master Chan. He and Jirugi. They want to attack us. We need to stop them.'

This brought laughter from the pirates. 'Cute. You two little ones. Against the army of Ming. I mean, points for bravery, but you know that's crazy? Anyway, we don't take passengers. If you come with us, you work. We're still few weeks away from landfall so there's plenty to do. No complaining. No slacking. Is that a deal?'

Bekko and Suki needed no discussion. This was clearly their safest option. Instinctively they trusted these pirates, despite the daylight robbery going on around them.

Bekko shook the hand she was offering. 'Agreed. Thank you . . . sorry, what is your name?'

'Rasmaya. Welcome to the Kunoichi.'

CHAPTER FIVE

'So, the Kunoichi are pirates?' Suki asked Somer, as they climbed onto the neighbouring ship.

'We prefer raiders for justice,' she shrugged, leading them below the deck. 'We steal from traders and deliver food to Sharan.'

'Where's that?' asked Bekko. He had never heard of such a place, despite studying maps of Gimandesh.

'It's a secret community on the coast. So many have been made homeless by Ming and his armies. He destroyed my mother's home and killed her family,' Somer explained. 'She's dedicated her life to helping all the people he has hurt. We train hard, we steal without killing. And we are always on the move.'

They came to a space filled with small hammocks.

'You can sleep here. I'll wake you up early so you can start work.'

Life on a pirate ship was tough. They soon discovered that everything was organized to a precise timetable. The pirates took turns to sleep, to clean, to cook, and to train. As they had no sailing experience, Suki and Bekko were given the simplest jobs to do. Everything on the ship was kept immaculately clean and tidy. There was a system for everything from folding sails to scrubbing the decks. Somer, who was second-in-command, took charge of their training and supervised their work.

'Kunoichi are the best sailors on these oceans,' she declared. 'But that is because we train hard and we don't allow sloppy attitudes. Suki, what have you done with that rope?'

'Er, I was trying to make it neat. It looked like it was in the way.' Suki said apologetically. 'Sorry, I was trying to tidy up as fast as possible. It looked tidy enough.'

'Hmmm. Enough is not enough. Let me show you. Pull that end, the one that attaches to the sail.' Somer showed Suki where to grab the line and Suki tugged it hard, expecting it to unravel quickly. She nearly fell over when it snagged on one of the rounded hooks attached to the high side of the ship.

Somer unhooked it and demonstrated how to coil the rope smoothly. 'If we were raising a sail that would have us in a heap of trouble. The line must run freely. Right now it might not matter if it sticks on the cleat there. Imagine if we were in a skirmish though, and trying to escape! It could be a disaster.'

Bekko wanted to understand more about how what was important to the pirates. 'When you say "enough is not enough" what do you mean?' he asked.

'It's something we always teach our crew. We don't like "OK", "more or less", or "good enough". That means there is room to do it better! We like thorough organization, proper tidiness, no short cuts. There really is no short cut to doing something properly. So every rope should be put away correctly. Every sail clean, mended, and folded. You have to take time to save time sometimes.'

Bekko listened carefully and then took the rope from Somer. He practised coiling it to run out properly. At first, he fumbled it. She helped him swing his arms to make long even turns. Suki and Bekko then took turns to set the line exactly like Somer.

'Your arms are shorter than ours,' Somer noted. 'That doesn't help. You are definitely improving though. Keep doing it. When you've improved enough then we can test it with a real sail.' She disappeared towards the stern to discuss the wind with Rasmaya, leaving the friends with the task.

Determined to master the skill, Suki and Bekko repeated coiling the rope. They didn't know that Somer was testing their discipline. Their shoulders started to ache. Their hands began to blister from skimming along the rope. Yet their warrior training had built good habits of resilience and obedience. Respecting that Somer was teaching them a lesson which needed practice, they stuck at it even when she disappeared below deck.

They weren't aware that she had posted another pirate to watch them from high in the crow's nest at the top of the mast. On and on they went, coiling and passing the rope.

'Impressive, aren't they?' Somer murmured to Rasmaya as she returned to the main deck. 'Great focus for such young monkeys.'

'They don't complain, and they try

to learn,' agreed Rasmaya. 'I like them. I still think they are crazy, heading off to Mahala with no weapons and no plan.'

'Hmmm. They said they had to start with no weapons.' Somer said, thoughtfully. 'I bet they'd be allowed to pick them up on the way though! Let's get them training with us tomorrow!'

'We've never taught Kunoichi skills to outsiders before, Somer.' Rasmaya seemed surprised. 'You really trust them that much?'

'Look at them.' Suki and Bekko might have been weary, but their work had not stopped. What's more, they were clearly encouraging each other and continuing to improve. 'Whatever training they have had in the past has made them great learners. We can help them.'

Decisively, Rasmaya nodded. 'Let's do it.'

In the morning, Bekko and Suki reported promptly for cleaning duties on the main deck. Still sore from their rope-handling on the previous day, they took the time to loosen up and stretch before they were due to begin scrubbing and polishing.

'Morning, shipmates!' Somer called cheerily as she came up from below decks. 'I have a challenge for you, are you up for it?'

'Bring it on!' Suki bounced up from

her stretch. 'I'm ready!'

Somer had to laugh at her enthusiasm. 'You don't know what it is yet!'

'Suki always loves a challenge.' Bekko explained.

'What about you, Bekko?' Somer asked, seeing he was more nervous than his friend.

'Warrior Monkeys know that facing a challenge is part of learning,' he told her. 'I'm more cautious than Suki but I always do my best. What do you want us to do?'

Somer was like Suki: naturally energetic and fearless. She could see Bekko's serious self-control, though, and respected it. As a leader, she valued different personalities in her team. And she was looking forward to seeing how the young warriors got on with pirate weapons training. 'How do feel about learning to use our slingshots?'

She opened one of the storage lockers at the side of the deck. Inside they could see rounded stones of all sizes, and several long thin ropes with a pouch in the middle.

'Ohhhhhhhhh! Cooooooooooooool!' Thrilled, Suki scampered round the deck and somersaulted with excitement. Bekko held the edge of the locker, looking down with fascination.

'This is how you attack ships on a raid? You knock them out with these? That must take a huge amount of practice.' He thought back to the bumped heads on the crew of the trader. Now it made sense. But to hurl stones so precisely across the water: that was a tremendous skill. 'How does it work?'

'Happy to demonstrate!' Somer picked up a slingshot, took a stone from the pile and tucked it deftly into the pouch. Taking a strong stance on the very edge of the deck, she whirled it several times around her head. It blurred into a continuous circle in the air until suddenly she let go of one end of the string. The stone flew through the air and they could see it land harmlessly in the water far away from the ship. Splash!

Suki was astounded. 'Amazing! Can

I try?'

'One step at a time. Can't have you chucking stones around without learning how to do this properly. Someone will get hurt. Maybe me! Here. Stand like this.' Somer showed them the best stance. It was similar to their stick fighting stance. 'We'll start with how you throw. Make sure your favourite hand is the one at the back. Swirl it round like this'

They enjoyed making circles overhead. Somer corrected their arm actions. 'If you use your wrist more it will help your accuracy when you throw. Hopefully, it won't matter much that your arms are shorter than ours.' She watched critically until happy with their action.

'Right,' she said, reaching for some slingshot strings. 'Now we'll add the string. And when that's going well I will let you throw these figs. That way you can't hurt anyone or break anything.'

The young monkeys were loving being out on the open sea with their new friend. And learning a new weapon really made it feel like an adventure. Having spent so many years training their physical skills and precision back at Senshi Castle, they were both pleased to find they were getting a feel for the slingshot quite quickly. Somer was pleased with them and let them splat lots of figs into the safe depths of the ocean.

'I think I've pretty much got it now!'

Suki was whizzing the rope around her head with great energy and enthusiasm. 'May I have a stone to test it properly?'

Somer shook her head. 'No way. Remember, enough is not enough. You are going to need to drill this a lot to get it right.'

Bekko was in no hurry to load up with stones. He was practising his throw and trying to get the fig to go where he wanted it. Sometimes he was miles off, but increasingly he felt he was finding the right lines. He was disappointed when Somer ended the lesson and went off to supervise the crew changeover.

Suki was ready for a break. 'Hey, Bekko, let's climb up to the crow's nest!

Rasmaya said we could as long as we don't bother the lookout.'

'You go ahead, Suki. I want to work on this some more.' He knew he was only a beginner. Yet the difference between beginner and expert was not luck. It was solid, mindful practice. He had found something he really wanted to master. The slingshot felt comfortable in his hand and the action was becoming natural to him. Now was a good time to keep drilling this new skill.

'OK,' said Suki, happily ditching her stack of figs and dropping her slingshot next to the locker.

'Hey!' hollered a junior pirate from further up the mast. 'Put that away properly! We don't want to be falling over your rubbish!'

'Oops!' Suki blushed and tidied everything up carefully. Bekko thought that living with pirates could be surprisingly good for her.

The pirates measured the ship's speed every hour using a log, which was dropped overboard. Bekko set himself to try and hit the log with his slingshot and figs. There was no doubt that he was missing it by a very long way. Fig after fig splashed into the sea; some too far; some too near; and some even flying off behind him. When Suki and Somer came back to find Bekko later, he was tired and sad.

'I just can't do it, Somer,' he sighed. 'I really have tried. Look how badly I miss. Can it really be done?'

For an answer, she took his slingshot and hit the very log he had just missed several times in a row despite it now being barely visible behind the ship. 'Yes. It can be done. But you might need to change how you are practising.'

'What do you mean? I'm trying to repeat the skill. I'm trying to look at what I'm doing and improve it every time. That's what Sensei Rika calls "mindful practice".' Bekko was a little offended that anyone could think he didn't know how to practise properly.

'That is all great. But when you miss

every time you get sad. And then you stop believing you can do it. So you get worse.' Somer started to tie little log targets to the edge of the ship. 'Here. Do you think you can hit this?' She indicated a biggish log, close to where they were standing.

'Sure. I think that will be easy.' Bekko replied. 'But if this were a raid, it wouldn't help at all if I could only shoot that far.'

'You're missing the point. When you can hit this one nine times out of ten then you'll be ready for something harder. We do this with everyone. If you set an easy target and smash it then you can move up a level. You get better and you stay motivated.' Somer watched Bekko hit the target several times in a row. 'Good. You need to keep track of how you're doing. Missing most of the time? Make it closer. Hitting most of the time? Make it further away.'

Suki could see how much better this would work for Bekko, especially as he often got upset and sad when he couldn't get the hang of something. She settled down to try it for herself. She rarely got frustrated like Bekko did; her habit was more to walk away and come back to it later. Still, maybe this would help her improve more quickly too. They both enjoyed counting their hits and changing to slightly harder targets. When the sun

was going down they cleared up every
last piece of fig, log, and string, leaving
the deck as perfectly tidy as when they
had begun. And as they swung in their
hammocks that night, Bekko dreamed
that Chan was floating in the sea with figs
splashing all around him.

CHAPTER SIX

'LAAAAAAAND AHOY!' came the
cry from the crow's nest. Their long
voyage was coming to an end. Their time
on the pirate ship had been full of new
experiences and hard training. Rasmaya
had given them plenty of food to start
them on their journey.

'You'll also need these,' she said,
presenting them with thick coats and
boots. 'Pack them away. One of the only

things we know about the trek to Mahala
is that it is colder than any place you have
ever been.'

'We don't have the words to thank you,
or any way to repay you for all that you
have done for us.' Bekko bowed low to
Rasmaya and her crew.

'The best way you can repay us is to
stop Ming. You go with our blessing. And
if you ever leave the Warrior Monkeys,
the Kunoichi would be proud to have
you in the crew. You will pass through
many different places on your way up
into the sky. The rebel community here
is called Sharan; that's where we are going
now. I'm sure if they can help you they
will, so be on the alert for friends as well

as enemies. Goodbye.' Rasmaya shook hands with Suki and Bekko.

Somer rowed them to the beach. It was very strange to stand on dry land again after so long at sea. 'I feel wobbly!' Suki laughed.

'You'll soon adjust,' Somer smiled. Then she gave them each a huge hug and a new slingshot. 'I'm going to miss you! Here, these are for you. Keep practising!'

They waved as she ran the dinghy back into the tumbling tide. Then they turned inland. Once again, they were on their own.

'So,' said Suki, despite them having repeated their plan a hundred times before leaving the Kunoichi. 'We trek into the mountains and find a way over. Then we go down to find Mahala on the far side.'

'Correct. Foothills first. Over there.' Bekko was already checking the position of the sun to help choose a path. Rasmaya had shown him how she used the sun and the stars to plot a course for her ship. Now Suki and Bekko could use this method on their long expedition into the sky. Hazy clouds hung over the horizon making it hard to tell what was hill and what was sky. They slung their backpacks and set off with very mixed feelings.

'I'm going to miss the pirates a lot,' said Suki sadly. 'It's good to think we are closer to Chan now though. I wonder how he is getting on? I hope they are treating him well.'

'I'm pretty sure that if they want him to train their warriors they will need to treat him well,' Bekko reassured her. 'Although, of course, they might be having a hard time persuading him. I don't think I envy them . . .'

Indeed, far off over the mountains, there was a lot of frustration in Ming's camp.

'Bring the prisoner to me!' Ming bellowed, scattering weasels as he threw his goblet to the ground.

'Yes, Your Imperial Highness. Straight away, Your Imperial Highness.' Bowing

and tripping over themselves, they all
dashed for the door. Out in the cold,
Chan sat cross-legged in a cage. His long
hair, usually wafting past his face, was
frozen into icicles. As serene as ever, he
opened his eyes as the cage door was
dragged open and the weasels surged in to
grab him.

'Hey, you. The Emperor wants to see you!'

'Again?' he sighed. 'Very well. Unhand me. I know the way.'

Nervously, they surrounded him as he glided across the snow towards the warmth of the Great Hall. He presented himself before Ming, with an incline of the head. It might have been a bow, or it might not. Either way, Ming proceeded with his interview.

'When will you complete the training? I am growing impatient with your excuses!'

'You surely don't want to use the troops until they are ready.' Chan was composed and firm. 'Many of the warriors were weak and needed time to get healthy again. They are making good progress now you have increased their rations as I suggested.'

Ming fidgeted with annoyance. He could see that what Chan said made sense, yet still, he felt as if it was some kind of trick. There always seemed to be some very important reason why the soldiers were not ready. Chan insisted all the troops had to learn to work together. He had made Ming build decent accommodation for them with warm fires and comfortable sleeping quarters. 'They cannot fight if they are not rested and well-fed.' When Ming resisted, Chan pointed out that he had been brought from the Shanti islands to produce a great army. If Ming wanted his advice, then it should be followed.

'OK, OK, so we wait. But there are other matters I must discuss with you.' Ming's irritation made his voice snappy and rude, though Chan remained as calm as ever. The ice was melting in his hair and dripping down his body as he stood in front of the throne. His quiet dignity contrasted with the sprawling panda.

'I am at your service, of course,' responded Master Chan politely. 'What other matters are these?'

'It's about your yoga,' Ming grunted.

'My yoga? What about it?' Chan raised an eyebrow. To a stranger, it might have looked enquiring. To those who knew him, there was some mischief in his expression. Almost as if he knew exactly what Ming was going to say. Almost as if this was part of a plan. Almost.

'Is it essential for you to chant so loudly at sunrise? It's disturbing me. I like to sleep until midday.' Once he had started grumbling, Ming couldn't stop himself, 'Two hours of chanting from 5 am until 7 am. Headstands. Handstands. Laughing exercises. Shouting exercises. It is ruining my day. Every day! It takes me ages to get back to sleep again.'

'My yoga routine is important for my health. I cannot train as I would like to

because you keep me in a cage. Surely you
need me to stay at my best?' Chan's face
was a perfect blank mask. Ming suspected
he was being teased . . . yet what the old
master was saying seemed legitimate.
'Perhaps you should move my cage
further away. Closer to the troops? Chan
suggested mildly, examining his icy toes.

'Never! You only speak to the troops
under MY supervision! I cannot trust
you.' Ming frowned. 'I suppose the yoga
will have to continue . . . My weasels have
been complaining though; it is not only
me who is disturbed by your antics.'

'They, and you, are most welcome
to join me. It is very bracing. Good
for the brain, you know. Especially

the headstands.' Chan opened his hands invitingly. 'We could start now, if you like?'

'No, no. I'm far too busy for all that. That will be all. Take him away!' Ming waved to the weasels, who scurried up to Chan ready to pull him away. A brief glance from Chan repelled them, and they made a circle around him as he departed smoothly.

They passed Hatti the elephant, dragging her logs to Ming's fireside. She bowed to him as he went and muttered something. He winked at her, unseen by his weasel guards.

'What was that?' they demanded. 'Why did she bow to you? What did she say?'

'Bow to me? She didn't bow to me, she just dropped something. I didn't hear her say anything. Perhaps she coughed?' Chan allowed himself a little smile as he was locked back into his tiny cage. Things were going well. Very well indeed.

On the other side of the mountains, Bekko and Suki were steadily making their way upwards. Already they were getting chilly and could feel a change in the air.

'Is it getting harder to breathe?' Suki asked Bekko. 'It feels weird.'

Bekko was relieved it wasn't only him. 'I feel puffed out,' he confessed. 'But I'm not tired. My head feels funny. What do we do?'

'Sit for a while.' The advice might have been well-timed, but they both jumped a mile.

'Who said that?' Suki blurted, looking around with alarm.

'I did.' Above them, a large black bird sat on a branch. He looked amused and relaxed. 'You must be Suki and Bekko. My name is Sam.'

From beneath his wing, another little head emerged. 'I'm Gil!' it squeaked, swinging upside down on the branch and waving a wing. Suki and Bekko flinched.

'Excuse us.' Bekko stammered. 'We fear birds. There are none on our island. In fact, the only time we have ever spoken

to a bird it tried to kill us.'

'I can see that would make this awkward,' shrugged Sam, flicking his talons with a wingtip. 'Well, we're not here to kill you. We're here to help.'

'Sorry, but how can we believe you?' said Suki, slightly shaken. Birds! She didn't *want* help from them. She watched as the little one tried to swing himself back up on the branch. He fell, but styled it out with a few somersaults and skidded into a heap next to them. Despite herself, she giggled. She guessed he was learning to fly.

'Smooth, Gil, very smooth, son.' Sam swooped casually from the branch and landed next to them with an elegant bow.

'I bring greetings from Rasmaya. I'm from the Sharan community.'

Relieved to be talking to a friend, Suki and Bekko quickly found that Sam knew an incredible amount. Firstly, he explained that they would need to stop every few hours to allow time to get used to the air.

'Breathe slowly and deeply,' he advised. 'You'll be OK, but you need to be patient.' He also showed them where to find more nuts and berries as their food stocks had got very low and they had been unsure about what was safe to eat as the vegetation was so different as they climbed higher. 'You're doing well, you've got a lot further up than I was expecting,' he said. 'Rasmaya and Somer told us you were tough. Let's hope you can conquer the mountains and rescue your teacher.'

'Thank you, Sam.' Bekko said, feeling warm inside at the thought that the Kunoichi had indeed sent some support as they had promised. It meant a lot to think they weren't alone. 'Is it far to the peak? How tough is the path ahead?'

Sam looked at them seriously. 'Yes, it is far, and it is tough. Soon you will be facing the snow and ice.'

'How do we get over the mountains?' Bekko asked. This had been worrying him more and more as they had caught glimpses of the steep white peaks ahead of them.

'You will need to take the Shinpi pass. It is very dangerous. Travelers often just disappear, never to be seen again.'

Bekko didn't like that much. 'Disappear?' he asked.

Gil jumped in. 'There is a huge voice hiding in the sky. And a snow monster! And the clouds attack the travellers! Tell them, Dad!'

'Ah that's nonsense,' his father chided, tutting at Gil. Then he shrugged expansively. 'Myself, I think it is just a very high and dangerous route. But it is your best chance.'

'Tell me something,' Suki wanted to

understand what they were facing, 'how does anyone survive in that cold? I can see the mountains ahead are all snow and ice. Does anything live there?'

'Monsters!' Gil burst again, flapping his wings excitedly. Sam swept him aside again with his huge shaggy wings, making him roll in a heap. 'Never mind monsters. Just keep going so you don't freeze. I don't think many creatures live there. I've never seen any.'

'That's a lot for us to think about,' Bekko shuddered. He was already finding the chilly air difficult. He was dreading the snow and ice ahead. 'We are very grateful for your advice. Thank you.' He and Suki bowed respectfully.

Sam rearranged his feathers and waved a polite wingtip. 'Well, friends, we salute you. Good luck with your mission.' He took a funny little run and launched himself into the air. He did some spectacular aerobatics while waiting for Gil to stagger up and join him in the air and they flew off upside down, much to Suki's entertainment.

'Well, they were brilliant!' she said. 'I wish they were going to be with us all the way.'

'We'd find it a bit hard to keep up with them,' Bekko pointed out. Already Sam and Gil were miles up in the sky and seemed to be dancing through the clouds.

'True!' she agreed. 'But thank goodness

Rasmaya sent them! Now we know where to go, at least. Though it sounds like it won't be easy.'

'It's a quest, it's not supposed to be easy! Here put your coat on now. We need to get going.' Bekko sounded very determined.

They both wrapped themselves in the thick coats, grateful for the extra warmth. Just for a moment, Suki was overcome with homesickness. She was scared, she was cold, she was hungry and she wished so much she could be sitting in Kuma's kitchen while he fussed over her messy hair and gave her fresh banana bread. A little tear crept out of her eye and she wiped it away quickly. She looked at

Bekko, fastening his coat, and already looking up the path ahead.

'Ready?' he asked, turning to her.

She nodded, scrambling up and stuffing her food into the bag. 'Let's go!'

Flakes of snow began to fall around them: a deadly blossom.

CHAPTER SEVEN

The next few days were bitter and harsh for the warrior friends. It was hard to stay cheerful when trudging through snow. Suki kept finding her head full of negative thoughts and it was getting harder and harder to keep them in. Bekko seemed very quiet and thoughtful as he always did, so it was a surprise to Suki when one morning he suddenly sat down and cried.

'I don't think I can do this, Suki. It's so hard!'

'Hey! Come on now! One step at a time. We just have to keep going. If we don't stop, we will get there in the end . . . you know that!' She tried to drag him up, but ended up slipping over and faceplanting in the snow. She sat up quickly, and as she shook the snow off her hair she had an idea. 'How about a game?'

'A game? Are you crazy? This is no time for a game!' Bekko looked at her angrily. Would she never take anything seriously?

'Fine, call it a challenge then. Remember how Sensei Rika says we always have to see the good? Well, let's practise.' She jumped up, and her energy helped him find his feet.

'OK then. You start. Tell me something bad,' he said, hoping it wasn't just going to make him feel worse.

Suki responded immediately. 'Sometimes I wish I could swap places with Nita! That's mean, isn't it? Imagine how she would hate it here!'

'That's easy! The good in that situation is that we're here together. If Nita was with me I would have pushed her off the mountain by now; she's so annoying!' That made them both laugh.

'Your turn!' said Suki.

'Hmmm, so many to choose from! OK,

here's one. I never imagined the snow trekking would be this hard. It's brutal up here.' Bekko shielded his face against another blast of snow that seemed to be attacking him.

'Yes, it is tough. We could never have known how tough it would be,' she agreed. 'I do think there's a good side though—when something is this tough it makes everything else seem easier. I don't think I'll be moaning about being cold and hungry ever again if we get through this.'

Bekko looked down. There was nothing to see there because the swirling mists made it impossible to see anything that was behind them. 'I keep thinking that every step takes us further away from home.'

Suki clapped her hands together triumphantly. 'Every step takes us closer to rescuing Chan.'

He grinned and held his hands up in surrender. 'You win!'

'KEEP . . . GOING!'

'Who said that?' Suki was startled. The voice didn't seem to come from anywhere. In fact, it seemed to be everywhere.

'Who said what?' Bekko had been wrapping his scarf around his head against the wind.

Suki grabbed his arm. 'I heard a voice! Just like Gil said!'

'I didn't hear anything. Are you sure you didn't imagine it?' Bekko looked concerned. Things were bad enough without magic voices. They listened hard. All they heard was the wind, so on they trudged, ever upwards.

Tiny ledges with huge drops on each side; rocky piles of boulders that could collapse with no warning; the path was getting worse all the time. They took turns to lead the way, hardly able to see each other through the constant blast of wind and snow hurling itself in their faces; hardly able to hear each other with the thunderous noise of a mountain storm.

It was a relief when the clouds lifted.

Bekko was puzzled to see large oval
marks in the fresh snow. They looked like
footprints, except they were far too big
for that . . . any creature with feet that
big would be a giant! He was about to
show them to Suki when she yelped with
excitement, jumping and pointing behind
Bekko.

'Look!' she cried. 'A gap!'

The horizon behind them showed a gap in the peaks. Exactly what they had been hoping for.

'It must be the Shinpi pass!' Bekko was suddenly hopeful. Was there an end in sight? 'If we zigzag back, we might be able to get up there by nightfall.'

'Look how close we are!' Suki shook some snow out of her hair and they turned with new hope towards the gap in the peaks. But then there was a sliding, juddering noise. The snow seemed to cough.

Startled, they looked around. Everything seemed to be the same. They shrugged and began to move again. Another squashy noise alarmed them and they paused. At that moment, an impossibly deep voice vibrated in their ears.

'STOP THERE. YOU HAVE TO GO BACK.'

Suki clutched Bekko's arm. 'Am I going crazy? Did you just hear something or was it in my head again?'

'No, I heard it too,' he said, looking around them frantically. 'But what was it?'

Another sigh in the snow and the ground seemed to slide downwards a little beneath their feet.

'That doesn't feel good . . . the voice said we should go back. But go back where? Do we go forwards or backwards?' Bekko was paralyzed with indecision.

'Can we trust the voice? Gil said it was a monster!' Suki looked up, down, all around. 'I'm scared, Bekko. Something feels very wrong here.'

'*HEY. GET OUT OF THE WAY.*'

'Come on, Bekko, let's try going back. Maybe the voice will say if that's wrong. Maybe it won't. But we can't stay here.' Suki grabbed Bekko's arm and started to drag him back where they had been.

'*FASTER NOW. IT'S COMING.*'

'I think I know what it is!' Bekko gasped as he and Suki battled along the ridge.

Suki had barely enough breath to ask

him, 'What?'

'Avalanche,' he puffed. 'Snow . . . collapses. Rolls down the hill. Oh quick, Suki!'

The snow seemed to swell and break like a wave rushing to the beach. Hearts in their mouth and lungs burning with the effort of scrambling through the snow, they tried to outrun it.

Suki was a little ahead so didn't immediately realize Bekko had fallen into thicker snow. When she looked back, panicked, he was miles behind, desperately racing the tumbling, rumbling, thundering avalanche.

'Go on, go on!' Bekko hollered, seeing that Suki was coming back for him. He

was almost swimming in his efforts to get away through the deep drift.

'I'm not leaving you behind!' she screamed, though the rapidly rolling snow was now far louder than her voice. Frantic as they were, the whole world seemed to slow down suddenly. Suki was stretching for Bekko; Bekko was nearly out of the drift . . . and then WHOOMPH! The avalanche hit. Everything sped up again and both monkeys were spinning in a strange freezing white earth. It was everything, and it was nothing. Then it was quiet.

CHAPTER EIGHT

Suki realied she must have fainted. Or was she dreaming? She was being carried. Something taking huge steps which crunched underfoot. Then it was dry, warm. No snow. The crackle of a fire and the smell of smoke. A soft blanket. She slept.

When she woke, she was drowsy and confused. She blinked, checking she really was awake. She was in a big cave

with a campfire at its entrance. Most of
the cave seemed to be occupied by . . .
a *thing*. It was not a bear. It was not a
monkey. Some kind of snow giant? He
had a shaggy, cheerful, friendly face and
seemed concerned for her. He handed her
a cup of hot soup. His voice was a deep
buzz, she guessed it was a giant whisper.
 'YOU OK?'

'Actually . . . I'm fine, thank you.' Suki felt better than she had for such a long time. She was warm and she felt safe. She sipped her soup; it tasted delicious. 'Where are we? And where is my friend?'

Her host pointed to a corner where Bekko was sleeping quietly. He looked very peaceful. *'HE WAS VERY BURIED. IT TOOK ME SOME TIME TO GET HIM.'*

'Should we wake him? Are you sure he is OK?' Suki was concerned, gradually remembering the horror of the avalanche and their desperate attempt to escape.

'HE VERY TIRED. HE NEED SLEEP. YOU ALSO VERY TIRED. SLEEPING TWO NIGHTS AND

DAYS. HUNGRY NOW, RIGHT?
MORE SOUP.' Her new friend refilled
the cup of broth that Suki had guzzled
without even noticing.

She realized she had forgotten her
manners. She bowed a formal greeting.
'My name is Suki, and my friend is
Bekko. We owe you a great debt.'

'MOUNTAIN IS DANGEROUS.
I TRY BUT CANNOT SAVE
EVERYONE. THEY DO NOT
ALWAYS LISTEN WHEN I TELL
THEM WHAT TO DO.'

'What is your name? And, sorry if
this is rude, but what are you?' Suki's
curiosity was reviving along with her
energy.

'*I AM A YETI,*' he shrugged. '*THAT IS THE GUY THAT LIVES IN THE SKY.*'

She smiled. 'Guy-in-the-sky. Thank you so much for saving us, Guy, and for looking after us.'

'*NO PROBLEM. AH, THE OTHER ONE IS WAKING UP. I GET SOUP FOR HIM.*'

'You're very kind,' Suki said. 'I'll go and see how he is feeling.'

Drowsy but rested, Bekko was amazed to find himself safe in a cosy cave with Suki. It was also incredible to have someone looking after them after such a long time of being brave and tough. The yeti was happy to let them rest while he went out to patrol. They kept the fire going and when he returned, they helped him make another soup with roots and berries he brought back from his excursion. Even though they were so far from the Shanti islands, they felt relaxed and at home. Night fell; they slept soundly in their new friend's home.

In the morning, they woke to find Guy was gone.

'Shall we go outside and look for him?' Suki suggested.

Bekko looked rather alarmed. 'What if we can't find our way back? And what if another avalanche should happen?'

'I'm a bit nervous, too,' she confessed. 'But we can't stay here forever. Let's just see if we can spot him.'

As it happened, they did not have to go far. The cave opened out onto the edge of a beautiful frozen lake. It seemed as if it had been scooped out of the top of the mountain ridge. The ice looked thick and solid . . . except for where the yeti had smashed a hole and was bathing peacefully.

Suki gawped. 'Look at him! Seriously, is he crazy? That must be soooooooooooo cold!'

'I don't know how he is doing it!' Bekko's face was a mixture of horror and admiration. 'Why would anyone try? How is he not freezing to death?'

'His fur is thicker than ours. Maybe

that helps?' Suki wondered. Though she couldn't help thinking the thickest fur in the world wouldn't be enough.

'GOOD MORNING!' The yeti noticed them on the edge of the lake. His voice reverberated around the lake. *'YOU COME TO BATHE?'*

Suki shook her head at him. 'I don't think so, Guy. We can't get in icy water. Too cold for monkeys!'

'ALL CAN BATHE. GOOD FOR BRAIN. GOOD FOR BODY. TRY.' Guy clambered out of the lake and shook himself off.

Suki inched cautiously across the ice and put one finger into the water where the yeti had bashed a hole to bathe himself. She took it out immediately, squealing with the cold.

'Careful, Suki.' Bekko urged her. 'Ice lakes are really dangerous. If you fall in, you might not be able to get out.'

'I AM HERE. YOU SAFE.'

'He's already saved our lives once, Bekko. He might be right. It looks awful but I want to try.' Suki was fascinated. It suited her reckless personality to try new things.

'Good grief, Suki-su. You are the craziest monkey I know. This time you are definitely on your own.' Bekko settled down by the lake shaking his head.

The yeti smashed a hole in the ice for

Suki. Without warning, she took a big breath and plunged in.

'AAAAAAAARGH!' she bellowed. 'Quick! Get me out!' Get me out!'

The yeti grabbed her and pulled her out; shivering and leaping with shock she rushed for her coat and wrapped it around her.

'NOT LIKE THAT,' he said. *'LIKE THIS.'*

He stood by the hole. They saw him take deep breaths and let the air trickle out slowly. He stepped into the water and, keeping the same slow deliberate breathing, he gradually lowered himself into the lake.

'He's doing warrior breathing,' said

Suki. 'Look, Bekko. Just like we do!'

Bekko could see the similarity. But still! 'It's a pretty extreme challenge, Suki.' He immediately wished he hadn't spoken. Suki loved nothing more than a challenge.

'Bring it on!' she growled. 'This time I'm staying in!'

She stood by the water. When she had done about thirty slow deep breaths she stepped in. It was horrible, awful, freezing, biting . . . but she breathed through the shock and made herself just take one breath at a time. This time she managed to stick it out for a few minutes.

'*GOOD. ENOUGH NOW FOR FIRST TIME. NOW OTHER MONKEY.*'

Suki pulled herself out of the water, tingling but glowing. Somehow, she felt great! 'Go on Bekko, try it. It's really good!'

'Oh, Suki. How can getting into freezing water feel good?' Bekko was very unsure.

'Hey, what about seeing the good?' she said. 'At the very worst, you'll be happy to get out again!'

'Ha. Well, that is certainly true.' He pulled his shoulders back and stood tall. 'Right. I'll do my best.'

'*SLOW.*'

'Yes, go slowly,' Suki encouraged. 'Warrior breath. Imagine it is pain. You can manage pain. And it's only cold, so not even as bad!'

Bekko tried to do exactly what the yeti had done. It took all his discipline not to squeal and protest about the cold. Slowly forced himself into the water. He tried pretending he wasn't even there. Instead, he imagined it was the warm sea by Senshi castle where he and Suki loved to swim. Then he found he was actually able to bring his mind to the lake, to the strange sensation of the chilly water. He found, suddenly, that he felt fantastic. Not only had he conquered the fear, but his whole body was also fizzing with energy. 'Wonderful!' he said, as he climbed out. 'That's so weird. I like it!'

'BRAVE MONKEYS. WILL BE

STRONG,' approved the yeti. 'LET'S EAT.'

'Sounds good to me, Guy!' Suki agreed, leaping and jumping all the way back to the cave. She felt ready for anything.

Bekko, too, felt refreshed and lively. Over breakfast, they explained to Guy where they needed to go.

'PANDA IS BAD,' he said seriously, shaking his head. 'DOES BAD THINGS.'

Bekko nodded. 'Yes, that's true. Our friend is a prisoner. We have to help him.'

Guy looked thoughtful and then his face cleared. 'I HAVE GOOD PLAN. YOU WILL GET THERE FAST. GET READY.'

They went to gather their bags and put

their warm coats on again. Bekko nudged Suki. 'He said "fast". Doesn't that sound alarming to you?'

She grinned. 'See the good, Bekko! Not "alarming" . . . try *exciting*!'

He rolled his eyes. 'I've got a bad feeling about this.'

The entrance to the cave was darkened by the big shape of the yeti returning. *'LET'S GO.'*

Suki ran out and gasped. 'AWESOME! Bekko, look! A sledge!'

Not just any sledge. A huge sledge, big enough for a yeti and at least twenty monkeys. Guy sat in and beckoned them to join him. Suki jumped in, highly delighted. Bekko took his place nervously; he held on tight to the back of the sledge. Guy leaned forward and the sledge seesawed . . . nose tipping downhill. It began to move, it gathered speed, and just like that, they were flying down the steep mountainside.

'Wheeeeeeeeeeeeeeeeeeeeee!' Suki

squealed. She had never travelled so fast in her whole life!

Whoooooosh!

They whizzed along, bouncing and bumping, sometimes even leaving the ground completely and crashing back down again. Suki loved it.

Bekko . . . not so much. Lurching around at a terrifying pace, he imagined how awful it would be to crash at such a speed. He felt sick. He shut his eyes, hoping it would be over quickly. He opened them again, wondering if he was going to be sick.

'Breathe, Bekko. Just breathe!' he told himself. Helter-skelter down the hill, they careered between peaks and cliffs. Bekko began to see how carefully Guy leaned from side to side to keep the sledge on a safe path. Ravines dropped away to one side; rocky areas seemed to stay away from them. Then, before Bekko could quite figure out how the yeti could steer so precisely, the snow was thinning, the air was warming, and they came to a stop. They looked down on a road winding towards a well-guarded wall.

'That's Mahala?' Bekko asked, in wonder. Were they really this close to Chan?

'BAD PANDA LIVE THERE.' Guy waited while they got off the sledge, rather wobbly after their journey. *'GO WELL.'*

Bekko and Suki hugged his legs and thanked him again. Smiling, he swung the sledge onto his back and set off to run back up the mountain, ready for his next rescue.

CHAPTER NINE

As the sun set over Ming's mountain
fortress, all was quiet after another busy
day's training. Ming himself had become
bored with watching the training and
now chose to stay in the comfort and
warmth of his throne room. He might
drift past a couple of times a day just to
check that Chan was working his soldiers
hard. He could see they were becoming
very skilful in their fighting. Fitter,

healthier, and happier, they thrived on the food and routine that Chan had insisted was essential. Ming was really looking forward to Jirugi's return to the court, knowing he would be able to show off an impressive army. It seemed their plan had worked well.

Chan was meditating quietly in his cage. He did not notice the nutshells flicking the ground in front of him. Suki and Bekko were trying to attract his attention, using their slingshots from a distant tree.

'It's no good,' grumbled Suki. 'He's just too zen. A few nutshells won't break his focus.'

'We could hit him?' Bekko suggested, tentatively. 'It wouldn't hurt with a nutshell but it might get his attention?'

'I've got a better idea, I think.' Suki rummaged in her backpack and found her notebook. 'Let's send a note.'

*Dear Master Chan. We are so happy
to see you alive and well. We have come
to bring you back to Senshi. We are
hiding but will seek an opportunity to
speak to you when it is safe.*

Your faithful students, Suki and Bekko.

She finished scribbling the note and
tied it to a stone. 'You throw it, Bekko.
You are better at this than I am.' Bekko
blessed his hours of practice on the pirate
ship. Taking careful aim, he flung the
stone into Chan's cage where it scuffed
across the floor and bumped into his
shin. They held their breath . . .

Chan half-opened his eyes. In the
failing light, they could not see exactly

what happened next. He barely seemed to move yet the wrapped stone was no longer visible by his legs. They had made contact!

'I just want to run over there and get him out!' Bekko's heart was bursting now they could actually see Chan after such a long and dangerous trek.

It was unusual for Suki to be the sensible one. 'I know, Bekko,' she said, squeezing his arm affectionately. 'I feel the same. However, we can't see where the guards are, or how the cage is locked. We can't just rush in. Imagine coming all this way just to get caught.'

'You're right,' he admitted, reluctantly. 'We wait. Oh, I hope we can speak to him tomorrow.'

'I'm sure we will find a way,' Suki felt strong and hopeful. 'We need to watch the camp and get an idea of where the guards are and what sort of routines there are. Then we can find the best time to plan the rescue! We're so close!'

They were too excited to sleep much and were in no way ready for the early morning chanting. It felt as if they had only been asleep for ten minutes. Suki couldn't help giggling. 'I bet Chan is only doing that to annoy them. He doesn't do it at home!'

Bekko was equally entertained. 'I'm so happy he seems so well. I hope they haven't been too awful to him.'

'Good morning, Suki and Bekko! Master Chan sends his greetings.'

Suki jumped so much she hit her head on the branch above. Bekko nearly fell out of the tree. Above them, a raven was looking down quizzically. She tucked her wings in neatly and continued. 'I'm glad to meet you. I heard you might be visiting. My name is Jamila.'

'Who told you we were coming?' Suki rubbed her head where a painful bump was appearing.

'We ravens have a network. Sam told us about your trek but we were not sure you would make it over the mountain.' She swept a feathery bow. 'Congratulations. Flying is a lot easier!'

'We had help. And luck. But how is Chan? Have they treated him badly?' Bekko asked, urgently. He couldn't bear to think of Ming hurting Chan.

Jamila croaked a little laugh. 'He is the most remarkable person I have ever met. I'm not sure he is even a prisoner. You cannot imprison someone whose mind remains free.'

Bekko was reassured. That did sound like Chan. 'Have they made him train the army?

'Yes, ' she replied. 'Ming is pleased with him and ready to impress Jirugi.'

'Oh no! So their plan worked?' Suki was disappointed. She wanted Chan to be safe but training the army of the enemy did seem to be a terrible price. The thought of Jirugi returning to the Shanti islands with a big army was very scary.

'I guess he had no choice, Suki,' Bekko reasoned. 'What else could he do?'

'I know,' she said, sadly. 'It just seems so weird that he would help Jirugi, that's all.'

'Jamila, can we see him? Can we talk to him?' Bekko asked the raven.

She nodded. 'There are lots of weasels patrolling the camp. His cage is very exposed so you can't go there. But when he takes training later he says if you wait in the trees over there he can try to slip away and talk to you then. The army drills are really loud and distracting so it will make a good cover.'

'OK, brilliant.' Suki was very excited.

Bekko felt a mixture of things all at once: happy, nervous, exhausted, and then suddenly . . . anxious. 'Do you think Master Chan will be angry with us for coming here?' he asked, suddenly. 'Maybe he doesn't need rescuing. Maybe he will think we should have stayed at home.'

'Angry? Oh, Bekko, do you really think so?' Suki's spirits dropped. If nothing else, she had assumed Chan would be pleased to see them. She remembered Sensei Rika saying Chan wouldn't need any help. Oh dear. Would their grand rescue quest all be for nothing?

Watching the assorted elephants, lions, tigers, and bears going through their drills with Chan was very sobering for Suki and Bekko. Now a huge force, they were disciplined and energetic.

'They look absolutely deadly,' Suki whispered to Bekko. 'Imagine if they attacked the Shanti Islands. We wouldn't have a chance. They are so strong! And look at how well they work together!'

Bekko had to admit he was terrified. This army had the potential to swamp the Warrior Monkeys. Brave as they were, they were no match for a powerful force like this.

Each instruction Chan gave was instantly carried out. Weapons drills, combat exercises, fitness training . . . this unit had all the skills and needed no reminders to train like they were already in battle. Ferocious shouts rang across the courtyards, perfectly organized troops crossed paths with leaping, climbing, and rolling exercises which seemed to depend on split-second timing. They had never seen anything quite like it.

'Look! That must be Ming!' Bekko nudged Suki, pointing to where the panda paraded across the training ground, surrounded by fawning weasels. He stopped for a few minutes to interrogate Chan about the training, then waved for his throne to be carried to the edge of the training ground. They could hear his high, lazy voice.

'I would like to see them line up for inspection,' commanded Ming.

'They have another five minutes to drill this section of their workout first,' said Chan firmly. 'Then they can line up.'

'Very well,' grumbled the panda. Why did that dratted monkey never just do as he was told?

Suki couldn't see where Chan had gone as the animals continued their highly coordinated routines. Then, suddenly, there he was, right in front of them.

'Well, well, young warriors. This is a very pleasant encounter. I had heard rumours you were on your way.'

They dropped out of the tree and rushed to embrace him. 'Master Chan! Oh we have missed you so much!'

'So much, that you have braved many dangers to get here.' He smiled down at them and their worries melted away.

'You're not cross with us for coming to find you?' Bekko asked, relieved beyond measure.

'Cross? Of course not! I am so proud of you both. What noble warriors you are becoming! I am deeply grateful for your loyalty. And I must confess, I will be very glad to go home to Senshi with you.' Chan looked wistful. 'The blossoms are so beautiful in my garden at this time of year, you know.'

'But, Master Chan, how can we help you escape?' Suki asked urgently, looking around them. Was that the beady eyes of a weasel she had seen in the bushes? It didn't feel like a safe place to talk.

'Escape, Suki?' Chan laughed gently. 'The time to leave has nearly arrived. In fact, I think . . .'

Whatever he thought, it was lost. Cackling weasels were popping out everywhere. 'SEIZE THEM! GRAB THEM! CATCH THEM QUICK!'

They were surrounded.

CHAPTER TEN

Suki and Bekko's faces were a picture of dismay. Chan looked as unflappable as ever. Absorbing the scene around them, he quietly pulled Suki and Bekko closer and walked back to the courtyard.

They were marched in front of the emperor where the whole army was lined up on parade. The nasty weasels, delighted to have new prisoners, nipped and snapped at the monkeys as they stood before Ming's throne. Ming was furious.

'I knew I could never trust you! This is a disgrace! No one gets away with disrespecting my authority. I've had enough of you. This is the end of your road, old man.'

'I have done nothing wrong. I was simply talking to these students. They came a long way to find me.' Chan seemed entirely unruffled by Ming's fury. Suki was looking defiant. Bekko was quaking inside but tried to look as composed as Master Chan.

The panda stamped his feet. 'Your students are not welcome here! And nor are you! You have outlived your usefulness. I've got the army I always wanted. I don't need you anymore.'

'Then we can go, and trouble you no further.' Chan bowed slightly and began to move backwards. Suki and Bekko did the same.

'There is no way that is going to work,' Suki breathed in Bekko's ear. 'We'd better be ready to fight.'

'Against this whole army? I don't like our chances very much,' Bekko whispered back, looking at the hordes of tough soldiers assembled for inspection.

The panda sat back majestically, throwing down his bamboo shoots. 'Ohhhhh no. You're going nowhere, monkeys. You know far too much about us and our plans. Guards! Execute them!'

Execution! Suki gulped and Bekko's eyes widened. They looked around for the guards but no one had moved. The troops seemed frozen in their places. There was a tense silence.

'GUARDS! DO AS I SAY!' Ming shook with rage, and his voice cracked a little.

At this, one of the soldiers moved. It was Hatti, the elephant. She stepped out of the ranks and slowly walked down to the front. She placed herself in front of the monkeys.

'This teacher has changed our lives,' she said in a clear but nervous voice. 'I had no help, no hope, and no happiness before he came. If you want to execute Master Chan, you will have to kill me first.'

'And me.' An old tiger stepped forward and joined her.

'And me.'

'And me.'

'And me.'

Bears, snow leopards, lions. All left
their places and pushed forward to defend
their teacher. Chan stood back with Suki
and Bekko and watched the drama unfold.

Ming was incandescent with fury. 'Get back in your lines! Do as you are told! You cannot disobey your emperor!'

Again Hatti stood her ground, supported and encouraged by her training buddies. 'Actually, we can. Because what you are doing is wrong. We want no part of it.'

'That's right!'

'She's telling the truth!'

'You're a terrible leader!'

Support came from all over the training ground.

'I think it's time to leave,' Chan murmured, taking a step back from the scene. 'My work here really is done. These animals are ready to rule themselves now.'

Hatti turned to them.

'Thank you for all your teachings, Master Chan,' she said. 'We will remember the way of the warrior. We will be kind. And we will always do our best.'

Chan bowed deeply, clearly touched by her words. The whole army clapped, cheered, roared and stamped their farewell as the Warrior Monkeys made their way towards the gate, ready for the long trek home.

Far up in the snowy mountains, a panda sat by an empty fireplace in an empty throne room. Even the weasels had run away from their master, once all his power had been taken from him. He looked up abruptly as the mandrill strode into the room.

'What on earth has happened here? Your report said you were confident the army was strong and loyal.' Jirugi was angry but mystified as to how the plan had backfired so badly.

'Oh Chan built a loyal army all right,' Ming spat back. 'Loyal to HIM! They've taken everything I had. Everything. It's all your fault. Why did I ever listen to you!'

'Me? You can't blame ME for this! You let this happen! I did everything that I promised. I can't believe you've lost my army, and my chance of revenge. You're pathetic!' Spinning on his heel, the

mandrill stormed out of the room leaving
Ming all alone.

The water garden was the perfect place
for Chan and Sensei Rika to talk about all
that had happened. The waterfall caught
the evening sunlight, sparkling as they
shared their news.

'I was afraid Bekko and Suki
wouldn't return,' Rika confessed. 'Such
endurance and boldness! The youngest
students ever to receive the blue belt of
the warrior!'

'They are young in age, perhaps,
but not in their actions.' Chan swished
his hair back, soaking up the wonderful
peace of being back in his favourite

garden. 'Look at all they have learned! You and I will not be here forever, Rika. We need future leaders with experience and sense.'

PING! SPLASH! PING! SPLASH! PING! SPLASH!

'WOOF! WOOF! WOOF!'

Clay bottles were skittled into the pond.

'Haha Bekko, I got more than you!' Suki, Bekko and Ishi raced into the garden, jumped into the pond to retrieve the bottles and raced off again, waving their slingshots.

'HEY! Come back here with my bottles!' Fara, the kitchen dragon, was giving chase, shaking her fist and breathing fire. She thumped through the garden in hot pursuit. They could hear still hear her voice. 'You pair of scallywags! Wait till I get hold of you!'

'Future leaders with . . . sense?' Sensei Rika enquired, smiling.

Chan sighed patiently. 'The warrior's path is not a straight one, Rika. Who knows what lies ahead for them? And for us? We choose to see the good. And to believe we can always keep improving.'

The yellow sun became orange, then slipped towards the horizon turning the whole sky pink and red. Chan and Rika watched their shadows lengthening as night fell softly over Senshi Castle.

BUILDING GOOD HABITS WITH THE WARRIOR MONKEYS

Habits are things you do without even thinking about it. Small changes can make big differences to your life: Warrior Monkeys try to make good habits and break bad habits.

Here are some examples of Suki and Bekko's warrior habits:

TIDINESS—It's much easier to find things if you put them away as soon as you finish using them. The pirates keep a tidy ship and take no excuses for messy behaviour! Suki really struggles with this.

PRACTICE—Regular practice makes a huge amount of difference to progress whether that is martial arts, music, or maths. Two minutes every day can be more powerful than two hours . . . if the two hours only happens when you feel like it. You don't have to want to do it; you just have to do it! Warrior Monkeys are experts at daily practice.

POSITIVE THINKING—
Finding the good in a
bad situation is a valuable
habit that can keep you
going when you need
motivation. This one is a
challenge for Bekko but
he tries very hard to work
on it.

HELPING—Doing chores as soon
as you are asked is a mature and
disciplined habit. This is another
way the Warrior Monkeys earn
respect and responsibility: they
get their jobs done quickly and
without complaining.

Good habits are hard
to make but easy to live
with. Bad habits are easy
to make but hard to live
with. Be like the Warrior
Monkeys and build great
habits, one day at a time.
Persevere and believe in
yourself. Good luck!